Meow
said the COW

Melardi

To Neil and Margaret Meacher, for all their love and support over the years. — E.D.

Text and illustrations copyright © 2009 by Emma Dodd

Library of Congress Cataloging-in-Publication Data

Dodd, Emma, 1969–
[Miaow said the cow]
Meow said the cow / Emma Dodd. — 1st American ed.
p. cm.
Summary: A noisy rooster causes a disgruntled cat to cast a magic spell that creates confusion among the other farm animals.
ISBN 978-0-545-31861-7 (hardcover : alk. paper) [1. Stories in rhyme. 2. Magic—Fiction. 3. Domestic animals—Fiction. 4. Animal sounds—Fiction. 5. Humorous stories.] I. Title.
PZ8.3.D636Me 2011
[E] —dc22

2010034247

10 9 8 7 6 5 4 3 2 1   11 12 13 14 15

First American edition, May 2011

Printed in China

The art for this book was created digitally.

Emma Dodd

Meow

said the **COW**

Arthur A. Levine Books
An Imprint of Scholastic Inc.

Early one morning, Cat was sleeping,
dreaming of hunting, stalking, and leaping,
when all of a sudden, out of the blue...

ck-a-
oodle-
doodle-doo!"

"This farm is **too noisy!**"
yawned the cat.
"Something needs to be
done about that."

Cat thought for a while and came up with a trick,
for he loved casting spells and doing magic.

When the sun rose next morning, all pink and red,
Rooster, as usual, threw back his head.
He puffed out his chest and opened his beak...

...and out came the tiniest,

"Squeak, squeak, squeak!"

"Ah-ha!" thought Cat,
with a sly little smirk.
"It seems that my spells
are beginning to work."

Pig woke next
and started yawning,
wanting his food,
as he did every morning.

He stretched his legs
and rolled in the muck,
then greedily grunted...

"Cluck

cluck, cluck!"

The hens got up and peered around — who was making that clucking sound?

It seemed to be coming from the sty...

Out in the field was more mischief from Cat –
the sheep were all barking, running this way and that!
Sheepdog was muddled – it seemed so bizarre –
his "woof" had gone missing,
he could only say "Baa!"

"**M E O W**," said the cow.

"Meow, meow!

What **has** that cat been up to now?"

The horse was quacking, the ducks were neighing –
nobody knew quite what they were saying!

Cat's clever plan had got out of hand.
The animals were louder than a big brass band!
So he crept away for a tasty snack –
a mouse or two from the old haystack.

By now the animals all could tell
that Cat was behind this beastly spell!
They were all feeling a little bit cross.
"It's time to show that cat who's boss!"

Suddenly, there was a deafening...

MOO!"

Cat was in trouble,
that much he knew.

Then **all** of the animals, small and big –
the mice and hens, the clucking pig,
the sheep and ducks, dog, cow, and horse,
and squeaking rooster too, of course –

chased that cat

right through the barn,

across the yard,

out of the farm.

Squeak! **Meow!**

Give us back **our** voices, **now!**"

What a noise they made
– a cacophony –
as they chased the cat
up the apple tree.

There really was
an awful din.
"OK," said Cat,
"you win, you win!
But you must admit,
it has been fun!"
With a flick of his tail,
the spells were undone.

All,
that is,
except
for
one...

Now every morning
it's Cat instead,
who opens his mouth
and throws back
his head...

"C

ock-a-
doodle-
doodle-
doodle-
doo!"

"Well," laugh the animals,
"that'll teach **you!**"